RICHARD UNGLIK

ANIMALS
OF THE WORLD

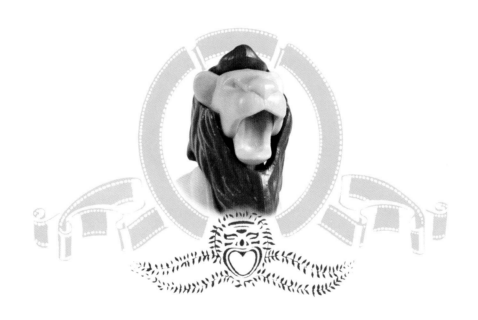

Dear readers,

In my first book, I took you on a journey around the globe to discover the people and cultures of the world. This time, we're going to discover the animals of the world, up close and personal.

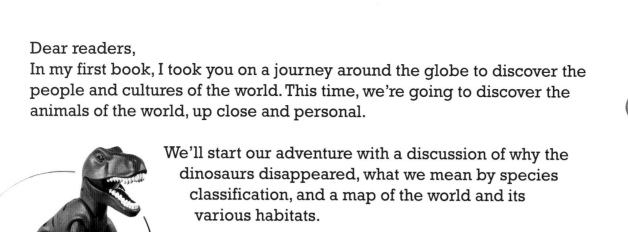

We'll start our adventure with a discussion of why the dinosaurs disappeared, what we mean by species classification, and a map of the world and its various habitats.

The first chapter is called Animals of History. We'll see that the history of humans and animals are often intertwined; not only in the story of Noah's ark, but also the legend of Hannibal's elephants, medieval animal stories, and the fables of La Fontaine. There are even animals who became movie stars and space explorers!

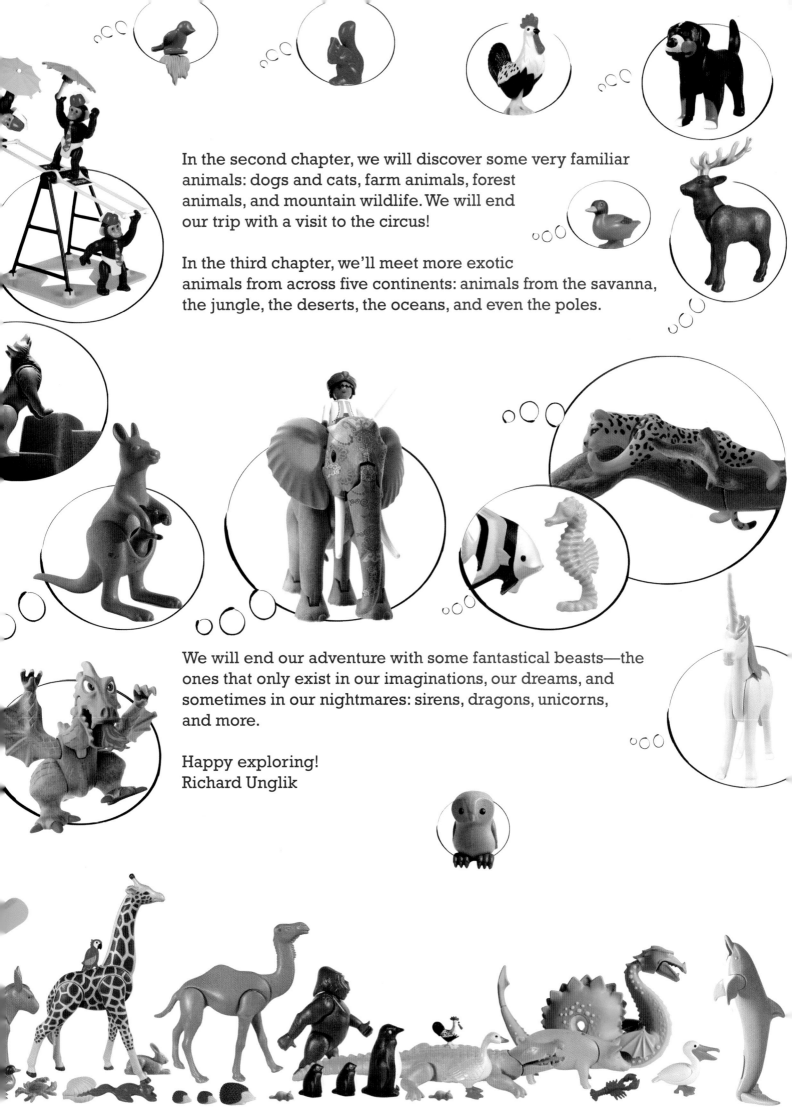

In the second chapter, we will discover some very familiar animals: dogs and cats, farm animals, forest animals, and mountain wildlife. We will end our trip with a visit to the circus!

In the third chapter, we'll meet more exotic animals from across five continents: animals from the savanna, the jungle, the deserts, the oceans, and even the poles.

We will end our adventure with some fantastical beasts—the ones that only exist in our imaginations, our dreams, and sometimes in our nightmares: sirens, dragons, unicorns, and more.

Happy exploring!
Richard Unglik

THE DINOSAURS

For 150 million years, they ruled the Earth. Some dinosaurs were peaceful herbivores, others were ferocious carnivores—but then, they disappeared, most likely because of a giant meteorite that created a gigantic cloud of dust.

The sky went dark, the plants disappeared, the herbivores starved, and then so did the carnivores. Finally free of its giants, the planet was left to the mammals, who began to thrive. This marks the distant beginnings of our history...

Major Species Classifications

Since the 19th century, we have classified animals into different species with a genus, a family, an order, and a class, depending on whether they have vertebrae; whether their blood is cold or warm; whether they swim, fly, crawl, or walk; and whether they eat meat or vegetables.

1) Vertebrates: These are animals with a spinal column (also called a backbone), and in general, two pairs of limbs. We distinguish between five principle classes of vertebrates: birds, amphibians, reptiles, mammals, and fish.

a) Birds are covered in feathers and lay eggs. Their wings allow them to fly (except for penguins, who swim), and their heads have a toothless beak. There are over 20,000 species of birds.

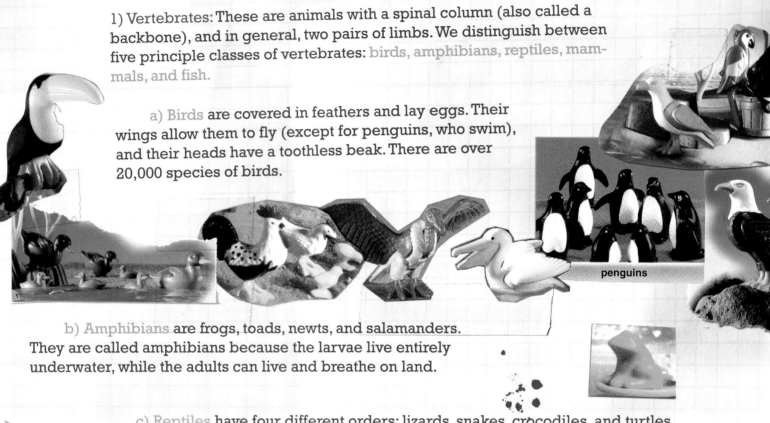

penguins

b) Amphibians are frogs, toads, newts, and salamanders. They are called amphibians because the larvae live entirely underwater, while the adults can live and breathe on land.

c) Reptiles have four different orders: lizards, snakes, crocodiles, and turtles. They are cold-blooded vertebrates that lay eggs and crawl. Most reptiles live on land, although some snakes prefer to live in trees. Crocodiles and turtles spend most of their time in the water.

crocodiles

turtles

d) Mammals have mammary glands, and their young are born without a shell. Mammals are grouped into several orders: primates, carnivores, ungulates (animals with hooves), insectivores, rodents, chiroptera (flying mammals), cetaceans, edentates, marsupials, and monotremes.

e) Fish are covered in scales, lay eggs, and move around using their fins. Some live in freshwater and others in the sea. They breathe underwater using gills, which pull oxygen from the water.

shark

2) Invertebrates: These are animals without a spinal column or backbone: insects, arachnids (spiders and scorpions), worms, shellfish, and octopuses.

octopus

The Mammals

Primates: The first order of mammals, the primates, include 188 species, from the tiny lemurs to the great apes—and even us, humans!

gorilla

chimpanzee

Insectivores: The mammals that feed on insects. The hedgehog is an insectivore.

Carnivores: They eat meat using their sharp teeth and claws. Dogs, wolves, cats, and even bears are carnivores, although some will also eat a lighter vegetarian meal every now and again.

dog and cat

brown bear and cubs

wolves

fox and cubs

tigers

Rodents: Rabbits and hares, squirrels, beavers, guinea pigs, mice, and rats are all rodents. They gnaw on plants with their long, sharp incisors.

Ungulates: Mammals with hooves. They are mostly herbivores.

cows

horses

moose

bison

elephants

pigs

Marsupials: Kangaroos and koalas are marsupials. They have a pocket made of skin where they keep their babies when they are born. Marsupials live in Australia.

kangaroos

Cetaceans: These are the sea mammals: dolphins, whales, toothed-whales, and killer whales. These (along with the great apes) are the cleverest beasts of the animal world.

orca

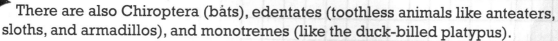

There are also Chiroptera (bats), edentates (toothless animals like anteaters, sloths, and armadillos), and monotremes (like the duck-billed platypus).

AMERICA

Hudson
Bay

Greenland

Iceland

Loch Ness

North
Sea

Copenhagen

EU

N

W   E

S

Atlantic Ocean

AFR

Great
Lakes

Mississippi

California

PLAYMO BIL PICTURE

Texas

Mexico

Cape Canaveral

Florida

Cuba

West Indies

Costa Rica

Tropic of Cancer

Canaries

Cabo Verde

Rabat

Marrakesh

Sahara

Gulf of Guinea

Equator

210   220   230   240   250   320   330   340   350   0

Pacific
Ocean

Amazon

Andes

Argentina

Rio de Janeiro

Tropic of Capricorn

Patagonia

The Wo

Finland

Russia

Siberia

ASIA

Mongolia

Black Sea

Caspian Sea

sylvania

Tigris

Tibet

Himalayas

Indus

China

Euphrates

Persia

Afghanistan

Katmandu

Ganges

Persian Gulf

Arabia

Gulf of Oman

India

Gulf of Bengal

Angkor

Ethiopia

Kilimanjaro

Lake Victoria

80   100   110   120   130   140

Indonesia

Madagascar

Indian Ocean

Australia

alahari

pe of
d Hope

Map of Animals

CHAPTER 1

ANIMALS THROUGH HISTORY

American Indians built totem poles to represent the animals that protected their villages.

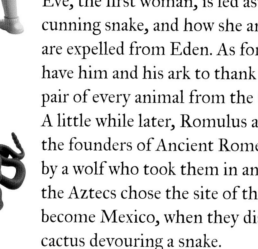

In the 16th century, the Aztecs founded their capital city Tenochtitlan (in modern day Mexico) on the spot where they saw an eagle devour a snake.

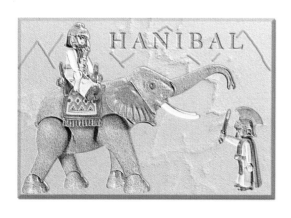

Almost every faith on Earth acknowledges that animals have walked with humans throughout history. In Genesis, God created the animals of the sea on the fourth day of creation and animals of the land on the fifth. Only then, on the sixth day, "He made Man according to his image." The Bible tells of how Eve, the first woman, is led astray by a cunning snake, and how she and Adam are expelled from Eden. As for Noah, we have him and his ark to thank for saving a pair of every animal from the Great Flood. A little while later, Romulus and Remus, the founders of Ancient Rome, were saved by a wolf who took them in and raised them. In America, the Aztecs chose the site of their capital city, in what would become Mexico, when they discovered an eagle perched on a cactus devouring a snake.

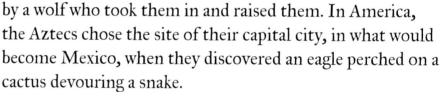

Making History

Some of our most amazing accomplishments would never have been possible without the help of the animals.

Over 10,000 years ago, the "Neolithic revolution" took place when humans domesticated dozens of species, including dogs, goats, sheep, cows, and horses. Attached to heavy carts or plows, the cows and horses helped people work the land and produce food. Hannibal, the bold, conquering soldier from Carthage, astonished his enemies when he crossed the Alps with his war elephants.

Ham, the first chimpanzee to be launched into space in 1961.

In the 20th century, humans went into space, but only after a dog, Laika, and a monkey, Ham, proved it was possible to survive an orbital flight around the Earth...

In 1697, Charles Perrault published the first written version of *Little Red Riding Hood.*

In Our Imagination

Our tales and legends, our stories and fables, and even our most modern films are full of animals who act a lot like us! Just think of the fables of La Fontaine, the tales written by the Brothers Grimm, the stories of Hans Christian Andersen or Perrault, or the legends of the Roman de Renart. There are also some humans we remember for their extraordinary ability to communicate with animals, such as Francis of Assisi, who talked to birds, and the Pied Piper of Hamelin, who lured the rats away.

Le Roman de Renart dates back to the 12th century.

Francis of Assisi (1182-1226) talking to birds.

The German legend of the Pied Piper of Hamelin was popularized in the 19th century by the Brothers Grimm.

A long time ago, according to the Bible, God wanted to punish humanity for its sins, and so He created a great flood to destroy all life on Earth. Only Noah and his family, because they were good and wise, would escape the apocalypse.

To save the innocent animals of the world, God ordered Noah to build a huge ark and collect a male and female pair of each animal alive on the Earth. For forty days and forty nights, the water poured down, quickly covering the whole Earth.

All living things died except Noah, his family, and the pairs of animals sheltered in the ark. When the waters finally subsided, they were able to repopulate the Earth and start over.

NOAH'S ARK

Quick! Quick! Hurry up! The water's rising!

*"Come and seek shelter in my ark!" shouts Noah
to the animals. "Time is running out!"*

WHEN ANIMALS WERE THE GODS OF MAN!

Most of the gods worshipped by the first humans took the form of animals. This was not religion in the modern sense, but rather animism (worshipping nature and animals), totemism (depictions of animal forms), or shamanism (entering a trance-like state and communicating through animals).

The Cro-Magnon men drew animals on the walls of prehistoric caves, most likely in order to worship them. For thousands of years, these beliefs could be found in many civilizations.

In Egypt, there are countless gods with the faces of animals, such as the falcon Horus, the cow Hathor, the wolf Anubis, the lioness Sekhmet. In Greece, they feared the Minotaur (a monster with a man's body and a bull's head).

In India, they praise the elephant god Ganesh. The native tribes had animalistic totem poles, and even the Hebrews, led by Moses, worshipped a golden calf in the desert.

As you can see, animals were the humans' gods long before they became humans' subjects.

A shaman dressed as a jaguar from Central America.

THE HORSE CONQUERS HISTORY

If the horse is considered the "noblest conquest of man," it is because this fine animal occupies a prominent place in our history. A symbol of power, speed, and mobility, the horse has been a domesticated beast since the dawn of Antiquity.

At first, the horse was simply a humble working animal, but then humans had the brilliant idea of climbing on their backs! From then on the horse would never cease to be part of the human story.

First there were the Romans with their mighty chariots, and then the Mongols, whose horses were small, but so powerful they could ride all the way to the edge of Europe. Then there were the Arabs on their proud thoroughbreds, and the knights on their chargers, dressed in armor as if they were castles themselves.

In the 15th century, Christopher Columbus introduced the horse to the New World. The natives had never seen an animal like it.

In the 19th century, horses carried Napoleon's French armies all the way across Europe to Moscow.

In America, the Wild West was the highest point of the relationship between horse and man. Can anyone imagine a cowboy without a horse?

In the 20th century, the invention of new, revolutionary transportation methods like the steam engine, also known as the "iron horse," and later, the car lessened the need to use horses for transportation. Nevertheless, most of us still have a special place in our hearts for our childhood heroes' most trusted companions.

THE FABLES OF LA FONTAINE

Who doesn't know at least one fable of La Fontaine? The fables, already familiar to many students in France, were written between 1668 and 1694, with education in mind. Jean de la Fontaine wanted to teach Louis XIV's heir how to recognize faults and different qualities in human beings.

A vast majority of the 244 fables written by La Fontaine feature animals small and large, wild and domesticated, frightening or friendly, sometimes smart, sometimes simple. The fables use animals to talk about human beings, describe their actions and personalities, and offer a moral conclusion.

Here are the most well-known animal stories:

Master Fox, the flatterer, asks Master Crow to sing so that the bird opens his beak and lets go of the cheese he is holding. The Wolf, mightiest of the mighty, devours the lamb, and teaches him that "might is right." Thanks to the Hare and the Tortoise, we know that "slow and steady wins the race." And because of Frog, who wants to become as strong as an Ox and ends up exploding, we know to reflect on the dangers of pride and vanity.

COME AND DISCOVER THE EXC...

BUFFAL...

RODEOS!

A STAGECOACH ATTACK!

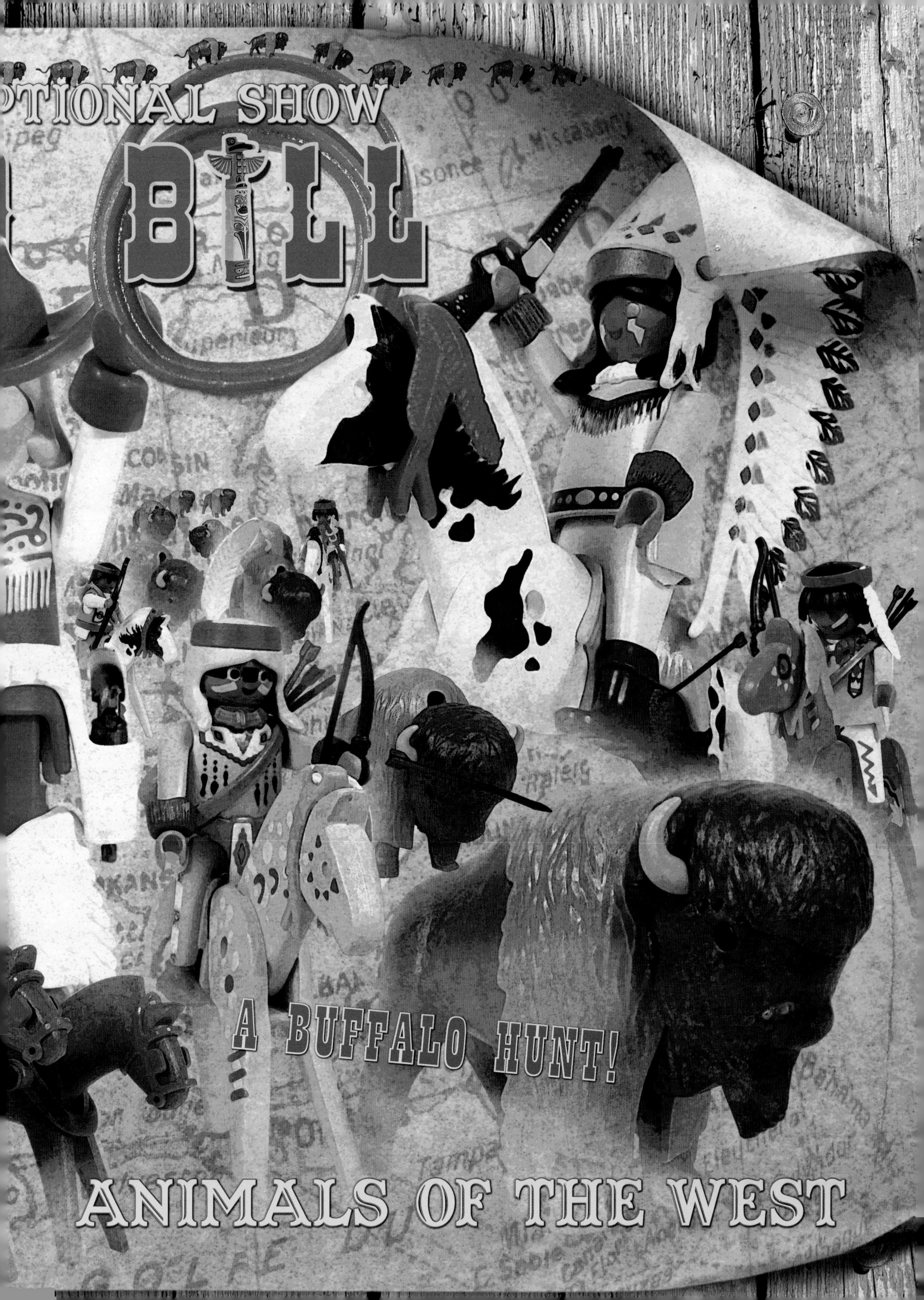
A BUFFALO HUNT!
ANIMALS OF THE WEST

Moby Dick

is the name of the white whale at the center of Herman Melville's novel of the same name, first published in London in 1851. We follow young Ishmael, who signs up to be a sailor on board the mysterious whaling boat, the Pequod. Its captain, a man called Ahab, is obsessed with Moby Dick, the huge animal who once took his leg. Since then, Ahab has only had one desire: to hunt down and kill the evasive underwater beast.

Adult sperm whales like Moby Dick are around 36 to 54 feet in length and weigh between 20 and 50 tons! Their jawbones contain about 50 teeth, each of which can weigh as much as 2 pounds! They primarily eat fish, of course, but also seals and sometimes even sharks. Their favorite prey is the giant squid, and the two animals can have ferocious fights.

KING KONG

Since the birth of cinema, animals have been seen everywhere in the movies. Our biggest celebrities should be jealous! You can see animals in all sorts of movies, but it's the fantastic and scary films that have inspired audiences and Hollywood directors most.

Ever since the release of King Kong in 1933, the most terrifying beasts have come alive in front of our eyes. Who didn't quiver when they saw Hitchcock's *The Birds, Jaws, Planet of the Apes,* or the incredible dinosaurs of *Jurassic Park*?

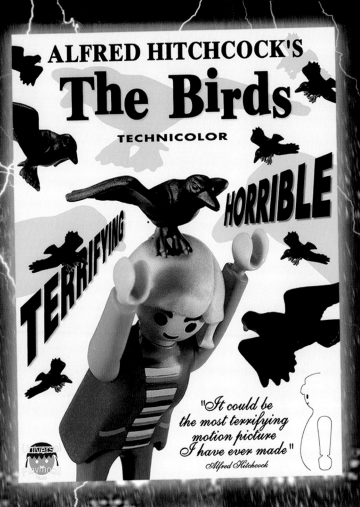

ALFRED HITCHCOCK'S
The Birds
TECHNICOLOR

TERRIFYING **HORRIBLE**

"It could be the most terrifying motion picture I have ever made"
Alfred Hitchcock

Universal
Playmobil
Studio

PLANET OF THE APES

The exciting and terrifying beasts of the

cinema!

JAWS

Universal
Playmobil
Studio

JURASSIC FUNPARK

CHAPTER 2

THE COMMON ANIMALS

In our cities, animals are everywhere. You only have to look up to see sparrows and pigeons flying by. (They're on the ground spying for breadcrumbs too!) Dogs have little room to run around in their doghouses or outside on their leashes. Loving comfort above all else, most cats don't leave the warmth of the house, except for a few adventures on the city roofs.

Service dogs help the blind. The master decides on the route, and the dog helps avoid the obstacles.

A Walk in the Woods

In the countryside and in the woods, animal life is still abundant, even if human activity and pollution are causing problems for some species. You can hear the owls in the dead of night and frogs and toads that croak by the side of a pond. Skunks make the most of their night to go hunting.

Frogs are the king of the pond (below). Perched high above, an owl spies its prey (below right).

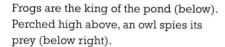

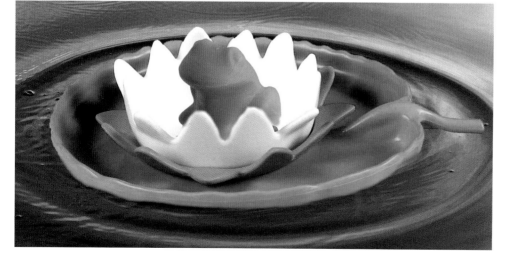

A Little Farther

Seaside, it's impossible to ignore the noisy seagulls who glide above our heads, and all of a sudden, plunge into the waves to catch fish.

In the heart of the forest, if you are quiet and patient, you may spot some of the animals who are very good at hiding: hares, deer, wild boar, and foxes.

Seagulls are coastal birds. They rarely venture out to sea.

To become a lion tamer, you need to be brave and patient. Learning to handle big cats can take many years!

Last but not least, those who aren't lucky enough to travel to where the animals live can go to the zoo or the circus to admire our animal friends: the tamed lions, the dancing elephants, or the monkeys who can juggle and roller skate!

Fine Dining

Let's celebrate all the animals, large and small, who provide us with the nutrition that is essential for our growth. Thanks to you, little pig, who gives us ham, bacon, and sausages. And hello to you, lovely cows, who give us milk, butter, and ground beef. Thank you, thank you, chicks and chickens, for your eggs and your roasted meat. Don't forget the fish, crabs, mussels, and shrimp that smell so delicious on our plates!

The Alley Cats

Domesticated animals that enjoy all the comforts of home, cats love a good pillow where they can purr near the heater. But felines also love their freedom strolling on the roofs at sunset! It's quiet up there, although sometimes they may encounter chimney sweeps, burglars, or romance...

Cats were domesticated 10,000 years ago, when the first farmers needed them to protect their barns from hungry rats and mice. Cats became precious, which is why, in the fertile valleys of the Euphrates and the Nile, they were worshiped like gods before becoming household pets.

In the middle ages, cats' lives became less pleasant. Beggars
and poor people saw them as a possible meal, and superstitious
people chased them away, thinking they were evil.

In the 19th century, with the spectacular growth of big cities,
cats came back into favor in the pretty houses of the
suburbs. Like their distant ancestors, they are
once again in charge of keeping away
the mice and rats.

Summer on the Farm

The best way to see animals is to spend the summer on a farm. What happiness! What activity! Hens peck on the ground, ducks quack loudly, and geese honk while the gander protects them from curious puppies. A mother duck and her ducklings paddle around the pond. And for the little pigs, it's feeding time! An owl has settled in the barn, hunting field mice hiding away in the straw.

Even with so many animals around, Grandma still finds time to take care of her cats and dogs, her doves, her cows and calves, her horse, her donkey, and a pack of small children who like to misbehave!

In the Mountain Pastures

During the summer, Hans loves to take the cows to graze in the mountain pastures with his grandfather. Under the watchful eye of Toby the dog, Hans plays with the rabbits and the groundhogs. Thousands of flowers fill the mountains with beautiful smells. Bees gather and feast on the pollen and will soon start making delicious honey.

In the Alps, cows are closely connected with the landscape. They are able to live over 10,000 feet above sea level, and are resistant to heat, cold, and thirst. Thanks to the large amount of milk they produce (over 8 gallons a day), the cow is an excellent cheese maker: Gruyère, Emmentaler, Vacherin, Beaufort, Tome, Reblochon, Raclette...Enough to fill many cheese plates!

A Traffic Jam in Corsica

Corsica is an island so beautiful that Ancient Greeks used to call it *Kalista*, "the most beautiful." Bringing great pleasure to its inhabitants and the many tourists, Corsica isn't just the Island of Beauty, as it's sometimes called in France. It is also a paradise for goats and wild pigs. It's quite common to see these free-roaming animals cause traffic jams on the mountain roads!

We are in Spain, at a bullfighting ring in Valencia. Dressed in his bright costume, Manuel is very proud. Today, it is his first public *corrida*, or "bullfight," and he mustn't disappoint the many fans who have come to see the show. The brass band announces the beginning of the fight, and the bull enters the ring. With his little red cape, called a *muleta*, the bullfighter (or *toreador*) must tire out the beast and lead it to the center of the arena. Every beautiful pass is greeted by shouts of "Olé!" from the crowd.

The Autumn Bellow

For the animals of the woodland, the deer's bellow is a sign that winter is on its wa
They all have to get busy: rabbits and hedgehogs prepare their burrows, squirrels collect hazelnuts, robins line their nests, and wild boars, along with their little ones, eat as many acorns as they can to grow fat for the cold months ahead.

When the field is cold, the grass is short, and the trees are bare, a strange army arrives from the gray skies of the countryside, loudly cawing. It is the crows.

O, lonesome black bird! You let us know that winter is coming, that time flies on, and that old age is just around the corner.

Beep Beep Beep Beep

Safely arrived in North Cape -stop-

Force 4 Storm -stop-

Very good fishing soles, sardines, and mackerels -stop-

Back in four days depending on storm -stop-

Beep Bee

Beep Beep Beep Beep

A Fishing Expedition in the North Sea

Whether the rain is pouring, the wind is blowing, or the snow is falling, the bold fishermen head to the seas on their small fishing boats. On board, everyone knows their job: one person drives the boat, making sure to avoid the big cargo ships they meet on their way; some maneuver the nets; and others empty the nets and sort out the fish.

To preserve the fish in the ocean, there are laws stating the minimum size of the fish to be caught. What if they catch fish that are too small? Easy, they go back into the sea!

Come closer, ladies, gentlemen, and most of all, children! Come and see the amazing parade of the circus animals! Marvel at the seals juggling hoops! Admire the skill of the horsewoman sitting atop her dancing horses! Laugh with our performing dogs, cats, and monkeys, who are the absolute best when it comes to misbehaving!

And what do you make of Jumbo and Dimbo, our dancing elephants? Last but not least, don't be frightened, our tigers and panthers are kind to their tamer!

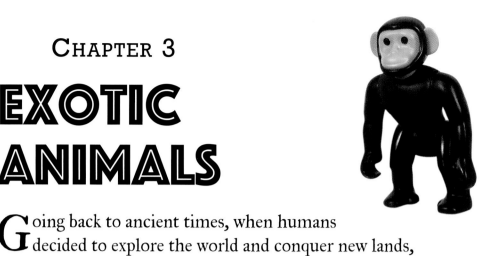

CHAPTER 3

EXOTIC ANIMALS

Going back to ancient times, when humans decided to explore the world and conquer new lands, there was a lot of fascination with the new animals that were discovered. Egypt's pharaohs brought back ostriches, giraffes, and parrots from their African expeditions, and the Romans introduced lions, monkeys, and extravagant peacocks to their Empire. In America, the Spanish conquistadors discovered llamas, eagles, and Andean condors and faced gigantic snakes and jaguars in the forests of the Amazon. Later, and farther north, pioneers and cowboys were shocked by the millions of buffalo living on the Great Plains of the Far West.

The majestic eagle, an American symbol, watches over its territory in the Rocky Mountains.

Jacques-Yves Cousteau (1910–1997). The books, films, and inventions of this Frenchman allowed many generations of kids to discover the marvelous world of the ocean.

Sea Creatures

Underneath the surface of the sea, in the "world of silence" held so dear by Jacques Cousteau, there is an unforgettable show to be seen. In the shallow water, there are lots of small fish, shellfish, and beautiful seahorses. Deeper, the dark waters of the abyss shelter unknown fish species, some of which can even produce their own light.

The giant panda lives in bamboo forests only in the center of China. Its name means "bear-cat."

The Charms of Asia

The vast Asian continent has an incredible diversity of animals. In India, elephants are used for work in the fields; every now and then they are painted with magnificent motifs and paraded down the streets for public holidays and religious ceremonies. Snake charmers hypnotize cobras to rise at the sound of their small flutes. In China, giant pandas try to survive, despite troubles from urbanization, pollution, and the hunters that threaten their existence. There are only about a thousand of them left in the wilderness. In order to protect these rare and fantastic creatures, a great natural reserve of 775 square miles was created and placed into the UNESCO World Heritage Program.

Australia is a world set apart: millions of years ago, it was attached to the single continental mass. However, once it became separated, the animals living there were cut off from the rest of the world and evolved in their own ways. This is why kangaroos, wombats, and koalas are only found in Australia.

Even at work, the Asian elephant is often painted with multicolored motifs. Strong, but stylish!

SERENADE BY MOONLIGHT

The howl of the wolves rings through the forest. The sound is enough to terrify even the bravest among us, to chill us all to the bone. That's because, for centuries, the wolf has been the most common villain of children's tales and legends. Their victims are countless! But these are just stories. The wolf is actually the most timid of all the big carnivores, and they are much more afraid of humans than we are of them!

Wolves are social animals that live in packs. A wolf pack has a very strict hierarchy. The wolves hunt as a pack, driving their prey toward the strongest wolves. This has been the inspiration for hunters since the dawn of hunting. Add an exceptional sense of sight, smell, and hearing, along with great stamina, and you get a particularly efficient big-game hunter. The pack will attack large animals like moose or reindeer without a moment's hesitation.

Wolves are fascinating, scary, and they even enrich our vocabulary! Here are a few expressions that show our admiration and fear of the wolf: "hungry as a wolf," "a wolf at the door," "have a wolf by the ears," and many more.

Of all the sea's inhabitants, dolphins are the most popular. Very friendly and sociable, they live in communities of around 100 members. Instead of having a leader, they hunt and defend each other as a collective group. They are believed to be extraordinarily intelligent. When they are not hunting, they take lots of time to play. Males, females, and babies—they all play together, jumping out of the water in perfect formation and making little whistling noises that sound like they're laughing.

Dolphins communicate using a variety of clicks and whistles. To move around and hunt, they use something called echolocation; they find out where objects are by calling out and listening for the echo. This means they can detect a school of fish from hundreds of yards away and navigate in the dark. Sometimes, human beings and dolphins work together when hunting. The dolphins find the fish and push them toward the fishing nets, where the fishermen are waiting to catch them.

THE KILLERS OF THE SEA

The Great White Shark is the most formidable predator of the ocean.

Up to 23 feet long and weighing around one ton of pure muscle, this is a shark designed to evoke terror. The Great White is most known for its tremendous jaw. With several rows of teeth that are automatically replaced when lost, the jaw can overcome any prey. Tuna and swordfish are often on the menu, but other sea mammals like sea lions, seals, and dolphins, as well as sea birds (and even other sharks!) may find themselves eaten. Any sea creature is potential prey for the Great White.

The shark lives a solitary existence in warm waters. It can be seen along the Pacific coastline, notably off the coast of California, Hawaii, and Australia where it terrorizes surfers. However, its reputation as a man-eater is blown out of proportion. Only a few dozen cases of Great White attacks have occurred in the last 50 years.

A WORLD OF SILENCE

These two adventurous scuba divers don't realize that the real treasure is the wonderful underwater world around them. The seafloor is packed with living treasures!

Thousands of multicolored fish and starfish swim among the seaweed and the coral. Seahorses watch the majestic octopus proudly show off its long tentacles covered in hundreds of suckers. Can it open the last-surviving bottle of port from this old shipwreck?

Meanwhile, crabs and lobsters share the bones of poor fish caught long ago. A lobster hides out in a cannon—he is waiting for an unlucky fish to pass by! The moray eel uses a similar tactic, but instead lies low on the sand hidden by seaweed and coral.

BANQUET ON THE ICE

The penguins of the Antarctic rarely gather as a family. While the mother sits on an egg, the father is off seeking food hundreds of miles away. When he gets back, it's the dad's turn to feed the little ones while the mom goes off to fish. Penguins don't have much family time!

A LITTLE BIT OF QUIET

The polar bear inhabits the south of the Arctic continent, all around the North Pole. When not hibernating, this solitary giant walks for many, many miles on the deserted ice fields, its nose to the wind, looking for food. Its exceptional sense of smell allows the bear to detect a seal from miles away.

Its body is particularly adapted to polar conditions. Its thick white fur protects it from water and the cold. Under its skin there is a thick layer of fat that allows the bear to float without getting cold in the sea. Polar bears are excellent swimmers, and they spend a lot of their time in icy waters. Unfortunately, polar bears are one of today's endangered species due to the threat of global warming. The ice fields used for hunting seals are growing smaller and thinner every year, and polar bears cannot access their prey until much later in the season.

CHAPTER 4

FANTASTIC CREATURES

Fantastic creatures are found everywhere in ancient mythologies, but they aren't really animals at all. Hybrid beasts with human chests and horse-like bodies, the Centaurs were feared for their fierce tempers and brutality. However, some of them were also wise and good, including the famous Centaur Chiron, who was the teacher of two ancient heroes, Achilles and Jason. On the other hand, you can expect nothing good from Cerberus. A dog with three heads, each packed with venom, Cerberus is the guardian of the underworld. Only the dead may enter, and no one can ever come back out. A hero named Hercules somehow manages to tame the fearsome beast...

Half man, half horse, the Centaurs are infamous characters in ancient mythology.

Monstrous and terrifying, Cerberus keeps the living from entering the underworld and prevents the dead from escaping. Beware his three heads, each with huge, venomous jaws!

The encounter between Ulysses and the sirens is a very famous section of the *Odyssey*, a work by the Greek poet Homer.

In the *Odyssey*, Ulysses and his traveling companions encounter sirens, horrible creatures with the tail of a fish but the head and arms of a woman. The sirens sing songs to lure sailors to jump into the sea and drown. Ulysses ruins their plans by covering his men's ears. He then ties himself to the mast of the ship so that he cannot throw himself into the sea!

The Little Mermaid, whose statue you can see in Copenhagen, Denmark, was made famous by the popular story by Hans Christian Andersen (1805–1875).

Sirens and Dragons

At the entrance to the port in Copenhagen, the statue of the Little Mermaid evokes memories for all the children of the world who remember the heroine of the famous Hans Christian Andersen tale, where a mermaid gives her life for the love of a handsome prince. Equally pleasant, the white unicorn immortalized by *The Lady and the Unicorn* tapestry, protects all the young girls who cross her path. Other creatures, sometimes frightening, sometimes friendly, are conjured up by our imaginations.

The Lady and the Unicorn is a French tapestry from the 15th century.

The waters of Loch Ness in Scotland are very dark, and the surroundings of the lake are often very foggy. Is that the reason why no one has ever seen Nessie up close?

Dragons are found in cultures across the world. In Europe, they are seen as terrifying, cruel animals, whereas in China they are generous, noble protectors. In the Chinese calendar, it is especially auspicious to be born during the year of the dragon, which comes around every twelve years. Yet another mystery exists: should we be scared of the yeti? For some, the abominable snowman is a cruel predator hiding out in the Himalayas. A savage beast, he only comes out when a snowstorm makes it impossible to see him clearly. He is apparently over 7 feet tall and his appearance is terrifying. But according to Tintin in Tibet, he isn't actually as bad as his reputation suggests. The same can be said for the Loch Ness monster in Scotland. If the creature exists, it has certainly never harmed anyone.

In the '60s, some people claimed to have seen a new fantastic animal: the pink elephant.

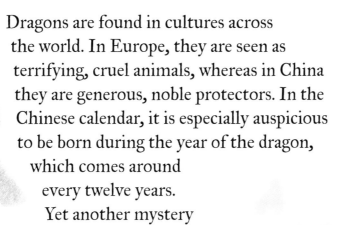

Once upon a time, the unicorns lived in the forest, close to water and rivers. Naturally shy creatures, they could never be approached by anyone other than the most pure and kind of young girls. Reassured, the unicorn would then lay its head in a young girl's lap and fall asleep.

According to legend, unicorns were hunted for their horns, which was said to be an antidote to poisons of all kinds. Some lords tried to capture the animal alive. But no one could hold a unicorn in captivity—too quickly, it would die from despair.

This fabulous white horse carries a single horn in the middle of its head, hence its name:

the Unicorn.

The Song of the Sirens

All the sailors of the world will tell you—at sea, the greatest danger
and the most beautiful of sights are the same, the sirens.

Sirens are gorgeous young women with the tail of a fish. They live at the bottom of the sea and only come to the surface to seduce lost sailors. They are so beautiful and their singing is so enchanting that sailors, unaware of the danger, abandon their ships and throw themselves into the sea to join the irresistible creatures. They are carried away into the abyss and never seen again.

The only thing we know for certain about Nessie, the

Loch Ness Monster,

is that he doesn't mind cold temperatures and he enjoys listening to bagpipe music.

October 1912 in the Scottish Highlands. It has been three weeks that John MacIntosh and Jack MacFly have been waiting on the banks of Loch Ness. They are trying to spot the legendary creature that's said to live in the deepest, darkest depths of these waters. But Nessie is shy and doesn't show up just like that!

In order to pass the time, Jack MacFly begins to play the bagpipes. Suddenly, Nessie appears through the fog! John MacIntosh manages to take a single picture. He is hoping it will be enough to clear the doubts of any skeptics.